I AM THANKFUL

We Pray, Pray, Pray Series

Written by: Carline Constant and Gregory Constant
Illustrated by: Leena Shariq

Subtitle: I AM THANKFUL.

For information contact us online at: www.sprinklejoybooks.com

Summary:

I AM THANKFUL takes us on a spiritual journey with Hanna, her little brother Caleb, and their grandmother. Grandma encourages her grandchildren to develop valuable praying habits to strengthen their relationship with God. Read on to find out what happens when Grandma falls ill and goes to the hospital. Will Hanna and Caleb embrace this challenging journey and continue to pray?

Subjects:
CYAC:: 1. Prayer Children's Christian Gratitude Realistic Fiction Book. 2. Faith Thanksgiving Books Children's Religious Christianity Realistic Fiction Book. 3. Godly Morals & Values-Prayerbook Gratitude Book. 4. Kids Giving Thanks To God-Picture Book. 5. Kids Spiritual Life Lessons-Christianity. 6. Raising Spiritual Kids-Praying Habits-Christian Picture Book. 7. Grateful Kids-Grandparent Christian Message Book. 8. Pray With Hanna Grandma & Caleb Christian Series-With Christian- Activities. 9. Christian Message Picture Book. 10. African American Christian Family-Realistic Fiction.

Identifiers:
Paperback ISBN # 979-8-9897681-6-5
Hardcover ISBN # 979-8-9897681-7-2
ebook ISBN # 979-8-9897681-6-5

Library of Congress Control Number: 2024911240

All scripture quotations marked (GNT) are from the Good News Bible Translation in Today's English Version-Copyright © 1993 by American Bible Society. Used by permission.

Printed in the United States of America
LCCN Imprint: Sprinkle Joy Publishing, New York.

10 9 8 7 6 5 4 3 2 1
First Edition: February 2024

Semi Realistic Art Style
For Ages 5-12

This book is a work of fiction, a product of the authors' imagination. Any similarities, references to characters, names, places, events, real people (living or dead), or real places are coincidental.

Sprinkle Joy Publishing Books

www.sprinklejoybooks.com

THIS BOOK
BELONGS TO:

____

WITH GRATEFUL HEARTS TO GOD!

To God be the glory!

****

This book is dedicated to my three sons, Gregory, Anthony, and Andy.

May God continue to mold and shape the three of you into responsible men.

Thanks to my family and friends for your words of encouragement.

Thanks to the editors for your contributions.

To all children and families worldwide.

-Carline Constant

Thanks to God for the many blessings.

-Gregory Constant

I AM THANKFUL

We Pray, Pray, Pray Series

Written by
Carline Constant and **Gregory Constant**

Sprinkle Joy
Publishing

I loved mornings. A new day meant new adventures.

The Little
Baby
Eagle

*But my most favorite thing about mornings
was getting to pray with my grandma!*

I kneeled beside Grandma and said,
"What should we pray for today?"

Grandma smiled. "Hanna, say what's in
your heart. God is always here to listen.
When you pray, say what you're thankful for
and remember how you care for others.
There's power in praying!"
Grandma bowed her head and said,
"God, I adore you. I thank you for keeping my
family safe."

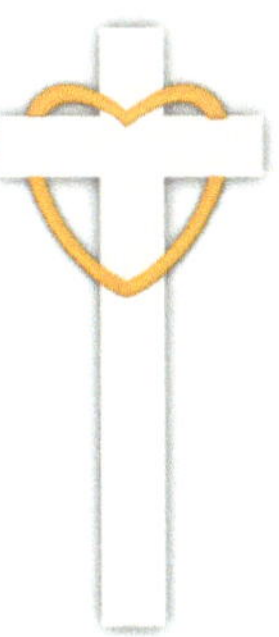

I bowed my head and prayed,

"God, thank you for my family and friends.

Thank you, for this day, for loving me,

and giving my family a home.

I thank you, God, for you are great."

What else am I thankful for? I thought.

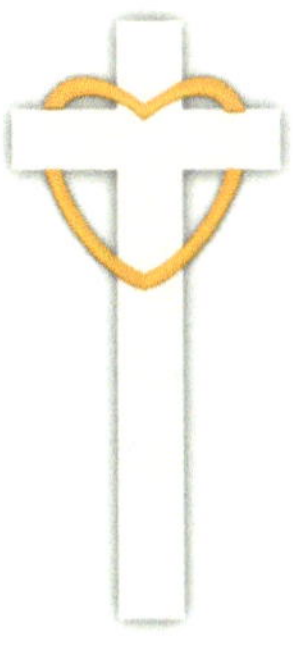

A memory from yesterday floated into my mind.

I had lost my hair bubbles and searched the whole

house for them for hours. My brother, Caleb,

helped me look for them. He found them

behind the couch and called out,

"I found your hair bubbles, Hanna!

They're a little sticky, but they still sparkle!"

I grinned and added to my prayer,

"Thank you for my little brother, Caleb,

who helps me and makes me laugh."

"Sweetie, that's beautiful," said Grandma.

Then, suddenly she started to cough.

"Are you okay?" I asked with concern.

"Fine, fine," Grandma said.

"Just a little tickle in my throat.

It must be allergies."

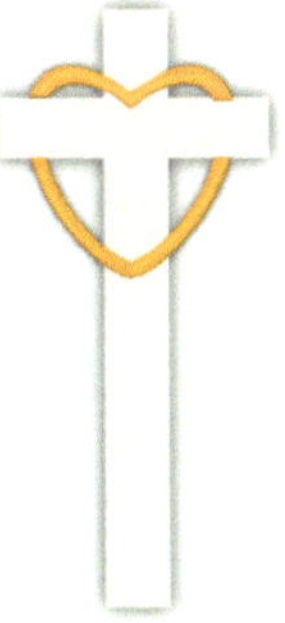

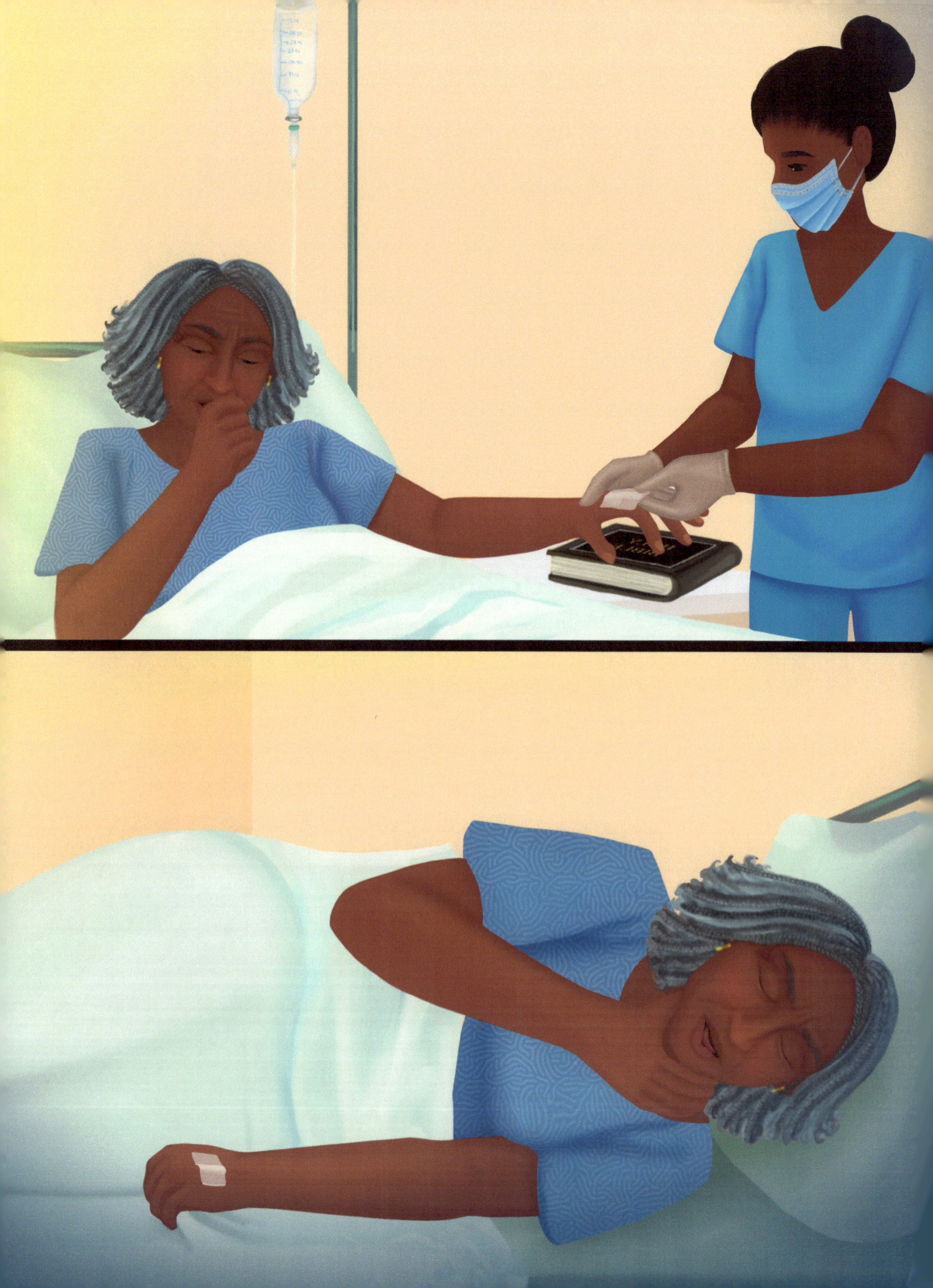

Later that night, Grandma's cough had gotten worse.

"I think we should take her to the hospital,"

Daddy told Mommy.

At the hospital, the doctor told us that Grandma was

ill with a bad cold and had a high fever.

I started to cry. *Grandma can't get sick!*

Who will I pray with in the mornings?

When we returned home, I sat in her favorite chair.

It smelled like Grandma's vanilla scent

and made me think of her kind words and soft voice.

I started to cry again. *I wished I could've stayed*

at the hospital with Grandma. I missed her so much.

I wished there was something I could do to help

make her better.

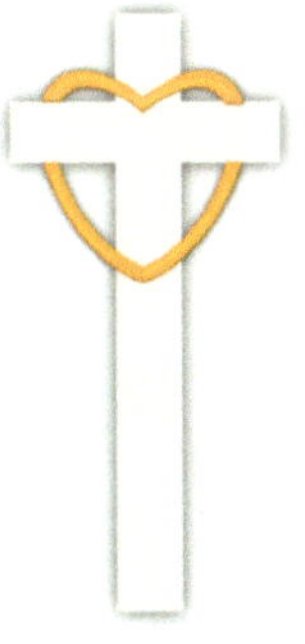

† AS FOR ME AND MY HOUSE, WE WILL SERVE THE LORD †

GOD, THANK YOU FOR TODAY.

In the morning, I didn't want to get out of bed.

For the first time, I didn't love the morning.

I didn't want to pray without Grandma here.

It wouldn't be the same. As I was walking down

the hall, I stopped when I found Caleb on his

knees praying like Grandma does, with his eyes

closed and hands folded. "Do not be afraid,

God is with you," he chanted.

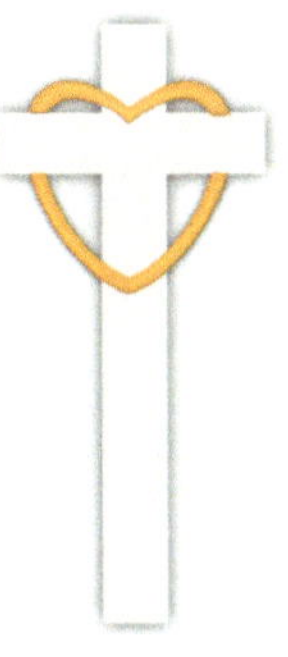

PRAY!
HEAL!
PRAY!
FIRST AID KIT

Caleb's words reminded me of a time when I

was riding my bike and I fell.

I scraped my arm and it hurt so badly.

Grandma held me and said, "Pray with me,

Hanna. God will make you well again.

God will heal your wounds."

She repeated these words over and over again.

My pain started to lessen, and in a few weeks

the wound was gone.

PRAY, PRAY, PRAY!
AS FOR ME AND MY HOUSE, WE WILL SERVE THE LORD

That's it! I know what I can do!

I can pray for Grandma to get better!

That's right. There's power in praying.

I walked into the room

and kneeled beside Caleb.

Maybe, if I prayed really loudly,

God would hear me and help her right away.

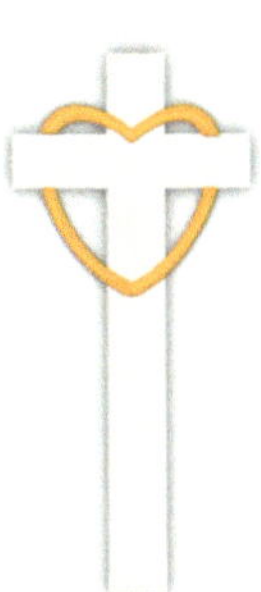

"God, thank you for Grandma!" I shouted.

"She's always ready to help anyone

who needs it and prays to you all the time!

She's amazing! Please, help her feel better!"

"Please, please, please!" Caleb added.

"We have hope in you, God," Mommy said.

"Help guide the doctors in her care,"

Daddy chimed in.

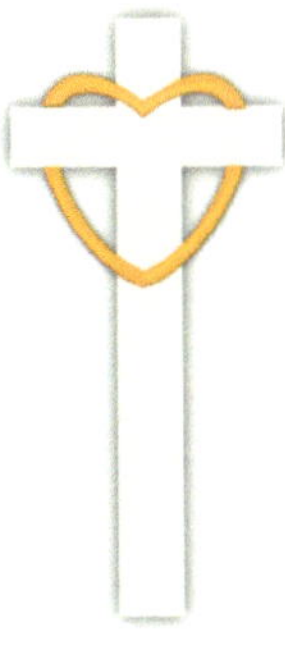

Days later, we visited Grandma in the hospital.

We walked into her room and found Grandma in bed.

"Bless you, God," she said.

"Thank you for your mercy and grace, God."

"Grandma's praying," I whispered.

I believed that God was listening and healing her.

As we came over to her bed, she greeted each of
 us with kisses and long hugs.

We showed her the gifts we'd brought

to cheer her up. Daddy brought her flowers and

Mommy made her favorite tea.

Caleb and I had created homemade cards.

"What wonderful surprises." She grinned.

"Thank you."

GOD BLESS YOU GRANDMA!

"We've been praying, Grandma," I told her.
"We've been praying for God to make you well again. I'd be so thankful."
She looked tired, but her voice was strong when she said, "May God bless my family, for you all are what I am most thankful for."
We embraced and hugged Grandma tightly.
Then, the doctor walked into the room.
"Your fever is gone," the doctor told Grandma.
"You can go home but continue to rest and drink more water."

"Thanks be to God,
who answers our prayers," Grandma declared.

That night, I prayed in my heart.
*God, I'm grateful for all you do
for me and my family.
Thank you for helping to heal Grandma.
You give me so much to be thankful for.*

Bible Verses:

"I thank you, Lord, with all my heart."

(Psalm 138:1 GNT)

"God will make you well again; God will heal your wounds."

(Jeremiah 30:17 GNT)

"Do not be afraid, I am with you!"

(Isaiah 41:10 GNT)

"Always give thanks for everything to God the Father."

(Ephesians 5:20 GNT)

"Be joyful always, pray at all times, be thankful in all circumstances."

(1 Thessalonians 5: 16-18 GNT)

"Give thanks to the Lord, because he is good, and his love is eternal."

(Psalms 118:1 GNT)

I PRAY TO GOD FOR YOU TODAY
PRAYER CARDS

I can **pray**! 😊   You can **pray**! 😊 😊   We can **pray**! 😊 😊 😊

*Write **prayers from your heart and/or Bible verses** on the prayer cards below. Color the outline of the cards with markers or crayons and present them as gifts to family, friends or anyone in need of a prayer.*

(sample) To: <u>Martha</u>
From: <u>Marie</u>
A PRAYER FOR YOU TODAY
I pray that God continues to give you peace and joy. Martha, thank you for praying for me and taking care of me when I was sick. I'm so grateful to have you as my sister, I love you.
(1 Thessalonians 5: 16-18 GNT) *"Rejoice always. Pray without ceasing. In all circumstances give thanks, for this is the will of God for you in Christ Jesus."*

To: ________________________
From: ________________________
A PRAYER FOR YOU TODAY

____
____
____
____
____

To: ________________________
From: ________________________
A PRAYER FOR YOU TODAY

____
____
____
____
____

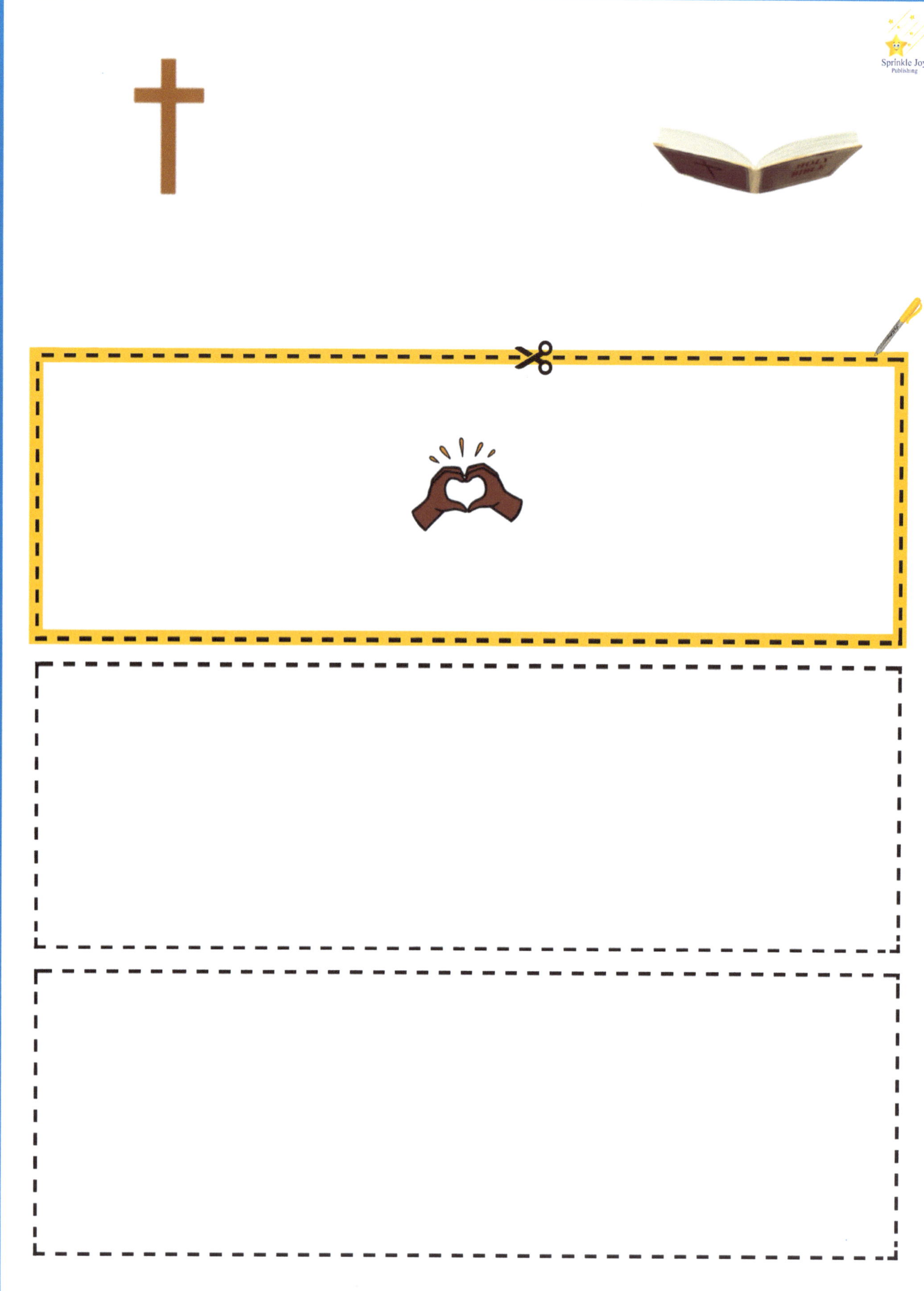

PRAYER WORD SEARCH

Directions: Find and circle the following hidden words.

APPRECIATE	GRATEFUL	CONFIDENT
BLESSING	PRAYER	GOD	THANKFUL
FAITHFUL	BIBLE	HOPE

T	C	I	V	N	Z	L	X	Y	M	B	P	H	G	I
P	U	Z	Q	C	O	O	X	G	O	Z	K	T	N	Y
L	B	J	O	M	G	H	O	S	B	P	G	I	G	Q
B	M	G	F	O	O	O	P	I	A	O	N	A	S	T
T	H	Q	J	P	J	O	O	G	D	D	U	F	B	S
D	H	A	E	T	F	L	O	Q	H	U	F	S	G	G
H	Y	A	Z	T	N	I	R	L	V	P	J	N	R	C
V	J	C	N	S	A	E	U	L	E	N	I	A	R	D
F	T	W	Y	K	B	I	D	U	A	S	T	E	I	R
N	N	D	U	I	F	J	C	I	S	E	Y	H	V	W
F	C	I	B	S	D	U	I	E	F	A	O	B	Q	I
L	N	L	N	H	E	X	L	U	R	N	E	X	O	D
A	E	P	I	S	B	B	L	P	G	P	O	I	L	A
W	Z	V	Z	P	V	N	S	J	F	E	P	C	G	G
X	D	Q	X	G	Q	Q	A	A	N	Q	X	A	N	P

PRAYER CROSSWORD PUZZLE

Directions: Complete the crossword puzzle below.
Use the following words across or down.

Confident   Faith   God   Prayer   Thankful   Hope
Grateful   Appreciate   Bible   Blessing

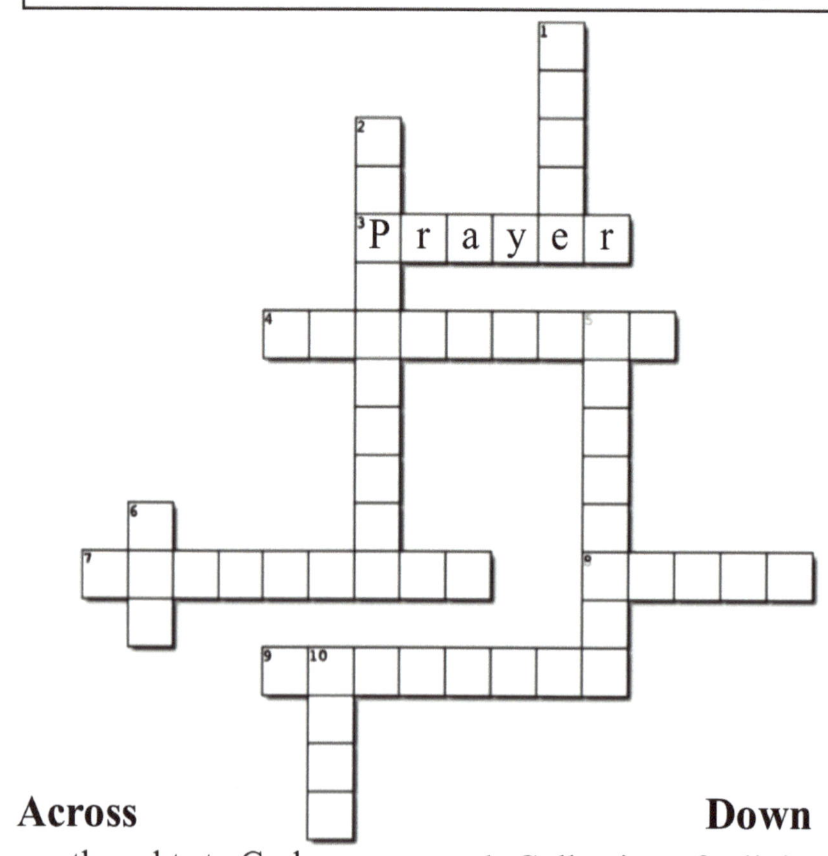

Across

3. We take our thoughts to God through ___________.(Prayer)

4. Favor and protection are God's ___________.

7. Having strong belief is to be ___________ in accepting and trusting.

8. When you believe, trust and have loyalty to God, you have ___________.

9. When we appreciate, we're also ___________.

Down

1. Collection of religious texts is a ___________ or scriptures that are sacred.

2. When you ___________ you're thankful, grateful and understand the importance of someone or something.

5. To be thankful and ___________, people appreciate blessings in life.

6. ___________ is our creator.

10. Having ___________ is to have faith in God's blessings.

WRITE YOUR OWN PRAYER TO GOD

<u>**Directions:**</u> **After reading or listening to** *I AM THANKFUL*, **write your own prayer to God. What are you thankful for?**
Remember to add details to clearly express yourself.
(Example: Dear God, I thank you for my mother, who takes care of me.)

Date:______________

Dear God,
____
____
____
____

Love,

____

*In the box below, draw and label a picture of yourself praying.

God, I thank you because…
____
____
____
____

 # WORDS TO KNOW 

Appreciate	To be thankful, grateful and understand the importance of someone or something.
Blessings	God's favor and protection.
Bible	A collection of religious texts or scriptures that are sacred.
Confident	To have strong belief, to accept and trust.
Faith	To believe, trust in and have loyalty to God.
Grateful	To be thankful and appreciate the blessings and good things in life.
God	The creator of people and things.
Hope	To have faith in God's promised blessings.
Prayer	Taking our thoughts to God and communicating with Him.
Thankful	To appreciate and be grateful.

About the Authors:

Carline Constant and Gregory Constant are a mother and son duo dedicated to spreading positivity through literature. They hope Sprinkle Joy Publishing books touch the hearts and minds of people everywhere. Each sentence, illustration and story telling idea of Sprinkle Joy Publishing books are made with love!

Carline Constant is a mother, author, and educator. She earned a Master's Degree in Education from Brooklyn College City University of New York.

Gregory Constant is an author, entrepreneur, and technology professional. He earned a Bachelor's Degree in Informatics from the State University of New York at Albany.

For information about Sprinkle Joy Publishing Books contact us online at:
www.sprinklejoybooks.com

About the Ilustrator:

Leena Shariq is a self-taught, Pakistan-based children's book Illustrator and Portrait Artist. Always encouraged by her parents, Leena started freelancing at the age of 16, and now, after only four years, she has illustrated many children's books, one after another.
Her body of work consists of semi realistic illustrations and stylised portraiture.

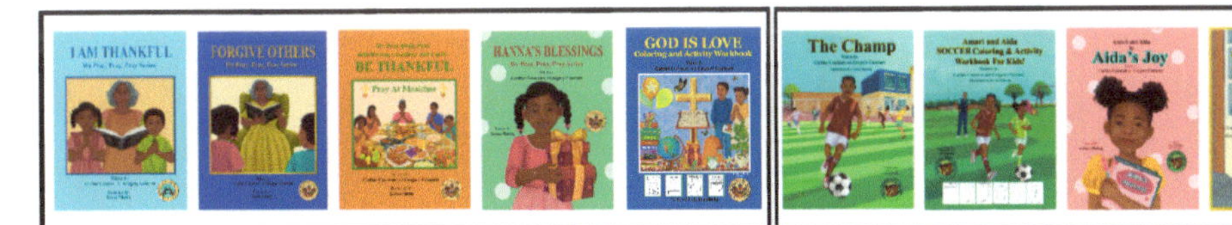

(We Pray With Hanna, Grandma, & Caleb Series)
I AM THANKFUL
FORGIVE OTHERS
BE THANKFUL: Pray at Mealtime
Hanna's Blessings
GOD IS LOVE Coloring and Activity Workbook

Also, by Sprinkle Joy Publishing Books
(Aida and Amari Series):
The Champ
Amari and Aida SOCCER Coloring and Activity Workbook for Kids!
Aida's Joy
Aida's First Day of School.
Amari Plays Basketball.
Amari and Aida in HOW TO PLAY BASKETBALL.
Aida Plays SOCCER. (coming soon)
Amari's Helping Hands (coming soon)
Amari and Aida in FUN TIME Coloring & Activity WORKBOOK For Kids!
Thanks to God for ALL!

Thank you for your purchase!
Please leave an honest review. We read every review
and they help new readers discover our books.

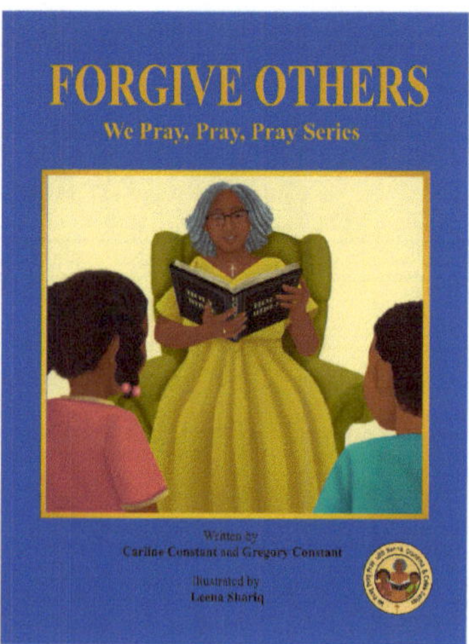

COMING SOON
We Pray With Hanna, Grandma & Caleb:
FORGIVE OTHERS.

Order Sprinkle Joy Publishing Books
www.sprinklejoybooks.com

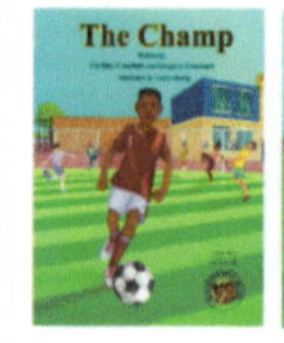      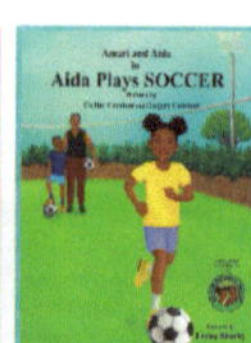

 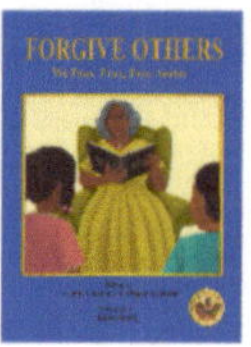 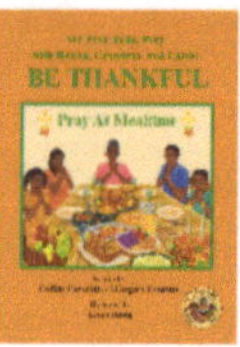 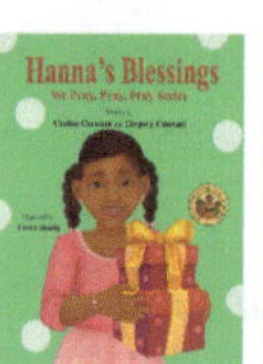 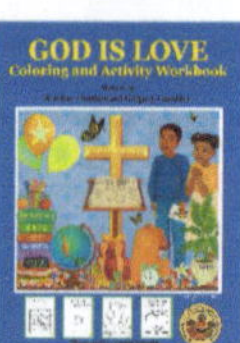

"PEACE
BE
WITH
YOU."

John 20:19 GNT